Another Constant
Friend
Pat
8/1993

CONSTANT FRIENDS

THE VICTORIAN
SCRAPBOOK OF

Ophelia B. Clise

BY MICHELE DURKSON CLISE
FOREWORD BY JONATHAN ETRA

VIKING
STUDIO
BOOKS

VIKING STUDIO BOOKS

Published by the Penguin Group

Viking Penguin, a division of Penguin Books USA Inc.,
375 Hudson Street, New York, New York 10014, U.S.A.

Penguin Books Ltd, 27 Wrights Lane,
London W8 5TZ, England

Penguin Books Australia Ltd, Ringwood,
Victoria, Australia

Penguin Books Canada Ltd, 10 Alcorn Avenue, Suite 300,
Toronto, Ontario, Canada M4V 3B2

Penguin Books (N.Z.) Ltd, 182-190 Wairau Road,
Auckland 10, New Zealand

Penguin Books Ltd, Registered Offices:
Harmondsworth, Middlesex, England

First published in 1992 by Viking Penguin,
a division of Penguin Books USA Inc.

10 9 8 7 6 5 4 3 2

LIBRARY OF CONGRESS CATALOGING IN PUBLICATION DATA

Clise, Michele Durkson.
    Constant friends / Michele Durkson Clise.
        p.   cm.
    ISBN 0–670–83285–0
    1. Friendship—Quotations, maxims, etc.   I. Title.
PNE084.F8C6 1992
177'.6—dc20   91–16755

Printed in Singapore

Especially for
Madeleine & Gabrielle

*T*here's nothing more comforting than friends. They always arrive just in time, like Popie and Marcello, to cheer us up with wild, impossible stories. They laugh at our jokes and pretend not to know the answer to questions we have asked two hundred times. When we mix up names and don't explain things, they understand. When we sound silly or don't make any sense, they know exactly what we mean.

Friends like Clarence or Conrad wouldn't dream of correcting us when we're wrong, or criticizing us when we raise our voice or refuse to eat the zucchini; they smile and nod and agree that zucchini is basically inedible. They always remember the good deeds we've done and ignore our mistakes. They politely consume our roast beef when it's burned. They adore the new lamp that doesn't work and the sofa that's too small. When our stock market tips collapse or we forget a birthday, it's all right. They bring flowers on a rainy morning. Ricky finds us the latest magazines, and baseball tickets when the game is completely sold out. And it is M. Ritz who comes up with the right little piece of blue tile to fill up the missing corner in the floor.

Who else but Ophelia has tea cakes and Earl Grey ready when we're lonely, no matter if it's teatime or 2 A.M.? If we break the crystal or upend the ferns, she knows how to fix it. Friends know what to do when the washing machine stops in the middle of the cycle—or at least they have the number of a good repairman. When the lights go out, there's Ophie with candles—scented ones to boot. When the cookbook falls behind the stove, she retrieves it (or can lend you another just as good or better).

In times of trouble, friends are solace. They're always around to comfort you, a shoulder to cry on and a hand to hold. On winter nights bears are the best thing to warm up your heart. They sit on your feet and nuzzle your nose. And, when everything is sunny and blue, friends share your joy. They go sailing with you and save the anchor. They go picnicking and, like Clarence, never forget the Dijon or Brie. They always invite you for Christmas, Thanksgiving, the Fourth of July. They never put you next to the kids—unless of course there's one you like. They never serve mashed potatoes with onion gravy, because they know how much it reminds you of Cleveland.

Friends endure us when we're grouchy or have nothing to say. They expect little and are so pleased with small favors. M. Ritz is delighted with ribbons, a funny card, or cheese and crackers in the afternoon with perhaps a scotch. We age, but Zenobia would never notice! In fact, friends tell us how fine we look, how much weight we've lost, how marvelous we are in beige.

Old friends don't disappear. Or if they do, it's to return one glorious day, like Conrad shouting and cheering at the back door with amazing presents—drums from Borneo, scarves from Chanel, a genuine matador's cape from Madrid. If they move away, friends write and call regularly. They send postcards from everywhere and photos once a month, cookies on birthdays, and a fruitcake for the holidays so heavy it must be unloaded with a fork-lift truck.

Finding new friends is like finding the perfect spring hat or shoes on sale at the best store in town. They're just right and you can't believe your luck. They're a joy and a wonder. They make you feel great and the whole world looks a lot better. Friends have new ideas and a different point of view, which makes ordinary experiences fresh and surprising. Suddenly just another day at the beach or a walk in the woods is an adventure. The movie you've seen a hundred times on TV seems brand-new.

Friends are a safe haven, a snug harbor for all inclement weather. They always take you in and never throw you out. You can't appear at Ophelia's too early in the morning or stay too late at night. Friends are a permanent part of your world, just as you are a cherished part of theirs. The time good friends spend together is the best part of life.

—Jonathan Etra

constant (kon'stent), *adj.* **1.** not changing or varying; uniform; regular; invariable. **2.** continuing without pause or letup; unceasing. **3.** regularly recurrent; continual; persistent. **4.** faithful; unswerving in love, devotion, etc. **5.** steadfast; firm in mind or purpose; resolute. —**Syn. 1.** unchanging, immutable, permanent. **2.** perpetual, unremitting, uninterrupted. **3.** incessant, ceaseless. See **continual. 4.** loyal, staunch, true. See **faithful. 5.** steady, unwavering, unswerving, unshaken.

friend (frend), *n.* **1.** a person attached to another by feelings of affection or personal regard. **2.** a person who gives assistance; a patron or supporter. —**Syn. 1.** comrade, chum, crony, confidant. See **acquaintance. 2.** backer, advocate. **3.** ally, associate, confrère, compatriot.

Bonne Fête

A proof of friendship's sacred tie
in these few lines you see
and often in some lonely hour
read and think of me.

Ophelia

2

Thank heaven,
the sun has gone in,
and I don't have to
go out and enjoy it!

Logan Pearsall Smith

Schnuff

Kind thoughts
come from the heart.
Ophelia B. Clise

Cheers! Ernest
VALENTINE
GREETINGS

"D'avantage est
rarement suffisant."

(More is rarely enough.)

—Ophelia B. Clise

3

Albert and Anemone

In days that come
and days that pass,
Let friendship
with us ever last.

Poli & Teddy

I am not of that feather
to shake off my friend
when he must need me.

William Shakespeare,
TIMON OF ATHENS

Dr. Churchill

There is a flower that grows
in every fertile spot
and if I remember,
'tis called "Forget-Me-Not"
—❧—

Zenobia

When you go out to parties
and don't get home till late
remember it is bedtime
and don't swing on the gate.

MUSIC

ACCORDION LESSONS
by ricky jaune

A Musical Evening
with
The charismatic Ambassador to Rome
Signor Marcello
Entertainments and La Dolce Vita
9 o'clock   May 7
R.S.V.P.

MARCELLO
*Ambassador
to Rome*

Improvisations pianissimo

Marcello

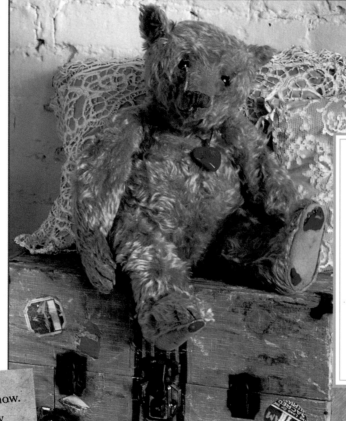

Aim at great neatness and simplicity. Shun finery and show. Be not in haste to follow new fashions. Remember that with regard to dress, bears ought to be decidedly plainer, and less showy than the people of the world.

Schnuffy

Though the world smiles on you blandly, let your friends be choice and few; choose your course, pursue it grandly and anchor what you pursue.

Dr. Churchill
as a young man

*Remember us early, remember us late,
and please give us a piece of
Christmas cake, or maybe two.*

Jon Etra

Teeny Bears at Christmas

The memory of my school days
is like a verdant bower.
Each one among my classmates,
a never fading flower.

My Circle of Bears

Sugar may melt
Flowers may die
Some may forget you
But never will I

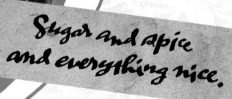

"I go to prepare a place for you."

12

Sugar and spice
and everything nice.

A Birthday Party

Heigh-ho for chocolate cake,
 nothing else will do.
Fudge is fine and spice is nice,
 but chocolate I save for you.

13

Ricky Jaune

For
Ricky
Jardire

BEST WISHES

BRADY B. BOEING

We cannot live on honey alone.

Japanese proverb

Brady Boeing and friend, Stella

14

As time rolls on and brings a change,
and friends from loved ones sever,
some may forget to think of thee,
but I'll forget thee never.

FIRST LESSONS
IN BEEKEEPING

IVY
CLINGS
LIKE
FRIENDSHIP
TRUE.

Christmas Greetings.

Brady Boeing

The heart that loves is always young

Frightening a piano into fits or murdering the King's French may be a good bait for certain kinds of fish, but they must be of that kind usually found in very shallow water. The surest way to secure a good husband is to cultivate those accomplishments which make a good wife.

Zenobia in her Bee goggles

ZENO BIA

Ophelia with mirror

As to Dress, decency is becoming to all, but extravagance opens a door to want; follow the fashion of the day as far as decency and good sense will approve, but avoid singularity. Be not troubled for what you have not; be thankful for, and take care of what you have. A Leghorn hat loaded with flowers, will not cure a headache, nor a gold watch prevent consumption.

American Farmer, 1860

A man of sense never exhibits haste.
Godey's Lady's Book 1860

PORTRAIT & LANDSCAPE
Photographer
AND
PICTURE FRAMER
J. Phillips,
SHORTMEAD STREET,
BIGGLESWADE.
CAMBRIDGE ROAD,
ST NEOTS.

COPIES MAY ALWAYS BE OBTAINED.
PICTURES OF EVERY DESCRIPTION COPIED, ENLARGED,
REDUCED & FINISHED
IN OIL WATER OR CRAYON.

Picture frames of every description made to order

I prefer to be where
there is no jostling.
Marcel Proust

Conrad

My very
dearest Zenobia
All the skies are
grey without
you

Your devoted
Conrad

Hotel Albemarle-Manheim
Brighton-by-the-Sea

Announces the Opening of the

Pompeian Fountain Room
on Terraced Roof

Edwina

Remember well
and don't forget
that you have a friend
in England yet
and in the Summer,
the North of Wales
and Scottish Coast.

Your friend Edwina

Dear Clarence,

It is not the same
here as it is there...
miss you. Bastille
day is not the same
without you.
I am very busy getting
organized for a new
project. Miss you.
More later.

Accept this rose,
my pledge of changeless love!

Love,
Clarence

Gently through the
sea of trouble
may thy life boat
smoothly glide

Clarence

Chocolate

Dilettante Chocolates™

Bears are constant, loving, adoring friends. They let you eat all the frosting from the cake.

21

Aunt Vita and Rollo with Cookies

Long may you live
Happy may you be.
Sitting in the garden
Thinking of me.

22

Randolph Fielding

LATE OF ALBERT STREET

Home Sweet Home

AMERICAN SCENERY

I prefer to be where there is no jostling.
Marcel Proust

Storms may blow
and waves may roar,
The house is warm
and we're indoors.
Home, Sweet Home

Jon Etra

23

*Albert and Anemone
and the Teeny Bears*

IN CELEBRATION OF SNOW
OPHELIA B. CLISE
INVITES YOU TO THE WONDER
OF A CHOCOLATE PARTY

SUNDAY EVENING
7 O'CLOCK

The superiority of chocolate, both for health and nourishment, will soon give it the same preference over tea and coffee in America, which it has in Spain.

Thomas Jefferson,
Letter to John Adams, 1785

Ophelia

Nor let us from these varied Scenes
of Strong enchantment part,
Till we have better learned to prize
the music of the heart.

Mona with bird

Questa casa e un paradiso
dopo lo strepito nelle trincee
This house is a paradise after
the din of the trenches
Spanish proverb

Sweet Home

Aunt Vita with Poli and Bijoux

Photograph of bearer

Keep diaries and memoranda of daily events and conversations, sermons, public meetings, beauties, wonders and mercies as you travel. Be minute and faithful. You never know when you'll need something inexpensive and interesting to read.

Bon Voyage

WITH
BEST WISHES

WITH
BEST WISHES

Backward, turn backward, O time in your flight,
make me a child again, just for tonight
Elizabeth Akers Allen
Rock Me to Sleep, Mother

Schnuffy

*If apples were pears,
and peaches were plums,
and the rose had a different name,
if tigers were bears,
and fingers were thumbs,
I'd love you just the same.*

Popie

30

Remember me when far away
and absent from sight,
and I will do the same for you
with pleasure and delight.

Mona

My love for you shall never fail
as long as there are seas,
as long as there are songs to sing,
but don't forget the cheese
Jon Etha

Ophelia and M. Ritz

C. M. Smith, 2310 Front Street, Seattle Wash.

We've been together so long, we're beginning to look like each other

Clarence and Ophelia

32

Do pop in for tea,
you are always
welcome any day
at 4 o'clock
A&A

The Tea Party

Under certain circumstances
there are few hours
more agreeable than the hour
dedicated to the ceremony
known as afternoon Tea

Henry James
The Portrait of a Lady

Hearts bound together,
by love's silver chain,
through life's roughest weather,
will faithful remain.

MI·GRO
EUX
es, Articles de Paris
AMEUBLEMENTS
S
RT
FUMEUR
he prix qu'en faorique

Moshe and Golda

In order to make reality more endurable we are obliged to encourage in ourselves a few small eccentricities — Marcel Proust

MAISON SPÉCIALE DE GRO
PARFUMERIE   Brosser
USTEN
DE C
C · AUB
22·24
Rue de Cursol
BORDEAUX   DÉPÔT
Des Parfumeries Françaises & Étrangères

35

Zenobia

Photo J. T. CLARKE Artist
STOCKTON ON TEES

IT IS A GREAT AND NOBLE THING TO EXCUSE THE FAILINGS OF A FRIEND; TO DRAW THE VEIL BEFORE HIS DEFECTS; AND TO DISPLAY HIS PERFECTIONS; TO BURY HIS WEAKNESS IN SILENCE, BUT TO PROCLAIM HIS VIRTUES UPON THE HOUSETOP.

Actress in 1922 Ophelia Role

ss Fuller and her two sis-
e folksongs of their vil-

J. D. Barr & Son
932 MARKET STREET,
Adjoining Baldwin Theatre.

Wholesale Store ❧ Factory, 323 Bush St.

TELEPHONE No. 3248.

PIONEER MANUFACTURERS
OF THE
LATEST STYLES
UMBRELLAS and PARASOLS

UMBRELLAS AND PARASOLS RE-COVERED AND REPAIRED

Canes Mounted

028720
AEROPORT
BORDEAUX

Ophelia

As to friends
who may call on you,
never be confused
or in a hurry;
treat them with
hospitality and
politeness,
and endeavor
to make them
happy.

Bedtime Bears

Jean de Noël

MONTE CARLO

Principauté de Monaco

38

Love is a golden thread
that binds
two hearts together.
If you don't break the
golden thread, we will
be friends forever.

Camille and Jean de Noël

Lives of great men all remind us
we can make our lives sublime,
and, departing, leave behind us
footprints on the sands of time.
Henry Wadsworth Longfellow
"A Psalm of Life"

Dr. Churchill

Served as Aide to Queen

Dr. Ernest Churchill
ENTOMOLOGIST, LEPIDOPTERA

after an exercise program and addi-

Matthews-Nelson

Dr. Longstaff
"Specimen."

As sure as the grass grows
around the stump
You are my darling
Sugar lump.
     Your Brother
     Rosario B. Elise

40

YUKIKO

SUGAR

Yukiko and M. Ritz

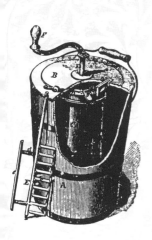

Ice cream, when properly made, is a modern luxury which in many respects has become as much of a necessity as tea and coffee. An entertainment, without this indispensable article, would be looked upon as almost a failure.

Godey's Lady's Book, 1860

Ophie, Aunt Vita and M. Ritz

FRIENDS EVER

OPHELIA'S WORLD
MICHELE DURKSON CLISE
RN65899
100% COTTON
HAND MADE IN CHINA

I loved Ophelia. Forty thousand brothers could not with all their quantity of love make up my sum.
William Shakespeare, Hamlet

Ophelia

42

It is my opinion that
the spirits of our lost friends
never leave us.
Madame Récamier

My friends

44

When the golden sun is sinking,
when your heart from care is free,
when o'er a thousand things you're thinking,
will you sometimes think of me?

*Camille
in her greatest role*

When mice come inside it is time to examine your winter wardrobe.

Japanese proverb

Education begins a gentleman, conversation completes him.

CONRAD

Conrad

46

With Best
Wishes
from Heidi von
Rosa &
Clafouti

Love does not consist in gazing at each other
but in looking together in the same direction.
Antoine de Saint-Exupéry

Heidi von Rosa
and Clafouti

Vita   "the twins"   Violet

Leaves may wither
flowers may die
friends may forget you
but never will I.

Clarence
my best friend

A C K N O W L E D G M E N T S

Constant friends are always with you, and mine have been a part of this book as well as my other books—Marsha and Michael Burns and their camera; Jon Etra and his humor; Tim Girvin, Stephen Pannone, Rachel Norton, and the staff at Tim Girvin Design, Inc., with all their time, talent, and generosity; Carol Leslie and her unfailing support and kindness; and Diane Millican and Nelly Myhre and customers of Bazaar des Bears,® whose good cheer and loyalty have all made these books a reality.

As new friends become old friends, I wish to thank Michael Fragnito for his continuing interest and faith, Barbara Williams for her patience and direction, and Martha Schueneman for keeping the bears on track.

To all of Ophelia's friends, I would like to tell of my delight that you have become a part of my world. As Ophelia herself would say, *"D'avantage est rarement suffisant,"* so please accept this little album as our keepsake of friendship.

Since before she can remember, Michele Durkson Clise has been drawn to antique and Victorian toys, especially "much-loved" teddy bears, which she began adopting more than twenty-five years ago. Her extended family of bears now numbers more than 100.

Michele Clise's bevy of bears have distinct personalities, and their exploits have been chronicled in her previous books: *My Circle of Bears, Ophelia's World, Ophelia's Voyage to Japan,* and *Ophelia's English Adventure*; her first book specially for children, *No Bad Bears,* will be published by Viking in 1992. Ophelia and her friends are also featured in Hallmark greeting cards, wall calendars, desk diaries, and jigsaw puzzles, and are the inspiration for Steiff's Ophelia and Schnuffy teddy bears.

For ten years, Ms. Clise owned Bazaar des Bears,® a gift and linens shop in Seattle's Pike Place Market that specialized in Victoriana. Before that, she was a commercial interior and window designer. She has also created a line of handmade bed and table linens named after Ophelia.

Michele Clise lives in Seattle, where she is currently working on more books as both author and producer.

Cover and book design by Tim Girvin Design, Inc.
Photographs by Marsha Burns.

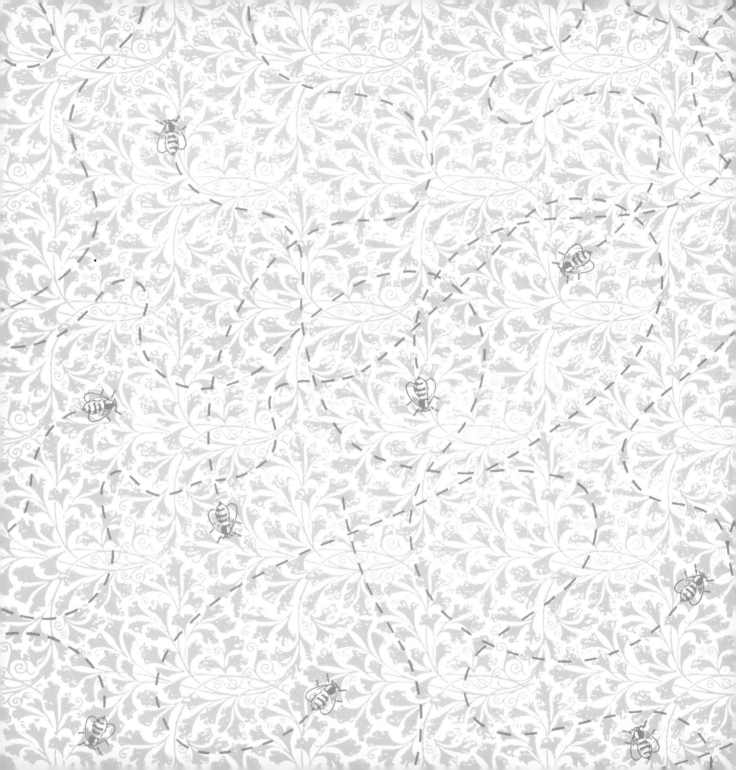